How To
Pray
Effectively
For Your
Spouse

CARLA STROGEN

CONTENTS

For the word of God is quick, and powerful, and sharper than any two-edged sword, piercing even to dividing asunder of soul and spirit, and of the joints and marrow, and is a discerner of the thought and intents of the heart.

Hebrews 4:12

FOREWORD

Our God abide by laws, statues and principles. No matter how sincere you pray, if you are not praying the word of God then you will not get the right results. So, I encourage you beloved to be effective in your prayer life. Get in God's word because the word works but, you must work the word in order to get results for your mate. For I am a living testimony of having a spouse that prays the word of God, and it has changed my life.

Prophet Sedirk Strogen
Sound Word Ministries, Inc

THE BEGINNING

26 Then God said, "Let us make man in our image, in our likeness, and let them rule over the fish of the sea and the birds of the air, over the livestock, over all the earth, and over all the creatures that move along the ground.

27 So God created man in his own image, in the image of God he created him; male and female he created them.

28 God blessed them, and said to them, "Be fruitful and increase in number; fulfil the earth and subdue it. Rule over the fish of the sea and the birds of the air and over every living creature that moves on the ground."

GENESIS 2:18-24

18 And the Lord God said, it is not good that the man should be alone; I will make him a help meet (helper suitable) for him.

19 And out of the ground the Lord God formed every beast of the field, and every fowl of the air; and brought them unto Adam to see what he would call them: and whatsoever Adam called every living creature, that was the name thereof.

20 And Adam gave names to all cattle, and to the fowl of the air, and to every beast of the field; but for Adam there was not found a help meet for him.

21 And the Lord God caused a deep sleep to fall upon Adam, and he slept: and he took one of his ribs, and closed up the flesh instead thereof;

22 And the rib, which the Lord God had taken from man, made he a woman, and brought her unto the man.

23 And Adam said, this is now bone of my bones, and flesh of my flesh; she shall be called Woman, because she was taken out of Man.

24 Therefore shall a man leave his father and his mother, and shall cleave unto his wife: and they shall be one flesh.

MATTHEW 19:4-6

4) He replied, have you never read that He made them from the beginning made them male and female.

5) And said, for this cause a man leave his father and mother and shall be cleave to his wife: and they twain shall be one flesh.

6) Wherefore they are no more twain, but one flesh. What therefore God hath joined together, let not man put asunder.

GOD'S ORIGINAL PLAN FOR MARRIAGE

GENESIS 2:21-24

21 And the Lord God caused a deep sleep to fall upon Adam, and he slept: and he took one of his ribs, and closed up the flesh instead thereof:

22) And the rib, which the Lord God had taken from man, made he a woman, and brought her unto the man.

23) And Adam said, this is now bone of my bones, and flesh of my flesh: she shall be called Woman, because she was taken out of Man.

24) Therefore, shall a man leave his father and his mother, and shall cleave unto his wife: and they shall be one flesh.

God designed sex between a man and woman to be enjoyed within the covenant of marriage. Marriage should be exciting and unifying. The husband and wife should serve each other, and meet each other's physical needs intimately to avoid temptation outside of the marriage. You should not demand from the other what is painful, harmful, degrading or distasteful to him or her.

1 CORINTHIANS 7:2-5

2 Nevertheless, to avoid fornications, let every man have his own wife, and let every woman have her own husband.

3 Let the husband render unto the wife due benevolence: and likewise, also the wife unto the husband.

KEYS TO ANSWERED PRAYER

Prayer is not optional, but it is essential for believers. This is the direct communication with God. The enemy would like to abort God's purpose, plan and destiny for your life. Don't give in, and give him the upper hand. Stand strong in the Lord and the power of his might. When you pray, you have to pray in faith knowing that God will answer. God wants us to ask with confidence, assurance knowing that we can go to Him about anything. When you pray in faith using the name of Jesus you are praying everything that his name represents. Something has to happen when you call his name.

Exodus 3:14

And God said unto Moses, I AM THAT I AM; and he said, thus thou say unto the children of Israel, I AM hath sent me unto you.

How do we get our prayers answered?

1) Let Your Request Be Made Known
2) Pray Effectual Prayers
3) Believe You Receive
4) Pray According To God's Will
5) Pray In Faith
6) Pray In The Name of Jesus

Let Your Request Be Made Known

Philippians **4:6,7**

6 Be careful for nothing, but in everything, by prayer and supplication with thanksgiving, let your request be made known to God.

7 And the peace of God which surpasses all understanding, shall keep your hearts and minds through Christ Jesus.

What is Prayer?

Prayer is communicating and interacting with God by requests, petitioning, and supplication for a need to be met.

What is Petition?

Petition- to ask or request.

What is Thanksgiving?

Thanksgiving – prayers of gratitude

Pray Effectual Prayers

James **5:16**

Confess your faults one to another, and pray one for another, that ye may be healed. The effectual fervent prayer of a righteous man availeth much.

What is effectual?

Effectual – to have power, to put something into operation, to achieve results.

What is fervent?

Fervent – zealous, eagerness of desire to accomplish or obtain something.

What is availeth much?

Availeth much – capable of producing results, prevails, to be strong.

Before something manifest on the outside, you have to see it on the inside first with the eyes of faith.

Believe You Receive

MARK 11:22-24

22 Have faith in God.

23 For verily, I say unto you that whosoever shall say unto this mountain, be thou removed and be thou cast int the sea and shall not doubt in his heart, but shall believe that those things which he saith shall come to pass, he shall have whatsoever he saith.

24 Therefore I say unto you, what things soever ye desire, when ye pray, believe that ye receive them, and ye shall have them.

Pray According To According God's Will

1 JOHN 5:14,15

14 This is the confidence we have in him, that if we ask anything according to his will, he hears us.

15 And is we know that he hears us whatsoever we ask, we know that we have the petitions that we desired of him.

Pray in faith.

Hebrews 11:6

6 Now without faith it is impossible to please him for he that cometh to God must believe that he is, and that he is a rewarder of them that diligently seek him.

Believe- to be firmly persuaded of the truth of something declared; expect or hope with confidence; to trust.

Pray in the name of Jesus

John 14:13,14

13 Whatever you ask in my name, I will do it so that the Father may be glorified in the Son.

14 If you ask me anything in my name, I will do it.

INTRODUCTION

God wants you to obtain wisdom, knowledge and gain understanding concerning your life that you may obtain the victory in all areas of your marriage. As you apply these principles by faith, then change has to take place. Once I searched the scriptures on these areas, I then applied them by mediating and confessing the word of God concerning marriage. He wants you to be victorious in all areas of your marriage. It is very important that you pray for and cover your spouse. You are to encourage and support one another. Show appreciation and give compliments, it does not take much to make someone feel special. One day, I sat down and realized I needed to learn how to pray more effectively for my spouse. So, I ask Holy Spirit to show me the scriptures that applied to husbands and wives. I began to write them down, and then applied them to my situations at hand. The word of God should be first and final authority in your life.

2 Timothy 3:16-17

16 All scripture is given by inspiration of God, and is profitable for doctrine, for reproof, for correction, for instruction in righteousness.

Psalm 1:2-3

2 But his delight is in the law of the Lord; and in his law doth he meditate day and night.

3 And he shall be like a tree planted by the rivers of water, that bringeth forth his fruit in his season; his leaf also shall not wither; and whatsoever he doeth shall prosper.

This is the only way to get effective results in making a difference in your life. Your situations will begin to line up and fall in place. The word of God makes the difference.

You have to be specific and pray consistently to see change take place in your marriage. I not only prayed scriptures for my spouse, but I prayed the word concerning myself. It was some things that I needed to get right. I still pray those scriptures for myself. God will begin to deal with issues that has not really been addressed. It is not to embarrass or condemn one another, but it is to pray and improve. You should want to do better, and grow up and mature in areas that need improvement in your life. God wants you to walk in freedom and liberty concerning your marriage. You can obtain the victory in every situation you face in your marriage.

Victory- with conquest, with defeat of an enemy or antagonist; triumphantly; as grace will carry us victoriously through all difficulties.

1 John 5:4

For everyone born of God overcomes the world. This is the victory that has overcome the world, even our faith.

Romans 8:31

What then shall we say to these things? If God be for us, who can be against us.

Romans 8:37

Nay, in all these things we are more than conquerors through him that loved us.

1 Corinthians 15:57

But thanks be to God, which giveth us the victory through our Lord Jesus Christ.

HINDERANCES TO YOUR PRAYERS

When it comes to communication in a marriage you have to think right, talk right and take the right choice of actions when disagreements occur. Words can be challenging, confrontational and argumentative depending on how you present it. Don't speak from your emotions when you are mad. At that moment you will say words that you don't mean to say, but because you are in the heat of the moment, you will say thing you don't really intend to say. Afterwards, you will realize, I should not have said that, or I should not have acted that way. The enemy want to bring strife and division into the home to keep you and your spouse at odds with each other as much as possible. Where there is no unity, there is no peace, but confusion in the home.

JAMES 3:16

16 For where envy and strife is, there is confusion and every evil work.

Don't allow strife to divide you, and don't allow conflict to remain between the two of you for long periods of time. Deal with the issue. You have to recognize the enemy does not have any new tactics. He will come with the same old baggage. If, the enemy can keep you divided there will be no growth and progress in the marriage. You are stronger together. It takes 100 percent from both to make the marriage work. Fifty, fifty will not work. It takes team work for a marriage to be successful. Marriage is not a fairytale. Dating and the honeymoon is a dream, but marriage will wake you up and face reality. Sometimes people are more concerned about investing more on the wedding day, and not willing to take the time to invest in the marriage. Marriage takes work. A lot of work. Be cognizant of how you handle one another. No, you will not always agree, but find a common ground to agree on. It's not about me or I, but it is about us working together. Sure, you both have said or will say the wrong words or shown wrong actions at some point in the marriage. Repent and apologize, and get it right. Don't walk around mad, and having attitudes with each other. Someone has to be the bigger person. Eventually the situation has to be resolved at some point. Show love for one another.

No matter how wrong you think your spouse is, you have to love anyway, and in spite of. Love forgives repeatedly. It forgives any offense. Satan does not want marriages to succeed. You have to put on your reinforcement, the armour of God to help during times of need.

Ephesians 6:12-18

12 For we wrestle not against flesh and blood, but against principalities, against powers, against rulers of darkness of this world, against spiritual wickedness in high places.

13 Wherefore take unto you the whole armour of God, that ye may be able to withstand in the evil day, and having down all, to stand.

14 Stand therefore, having your loins girt about with truth, and having on the breastplate of righteousness;

15 And your feet shod with the preparation of the gospel of peace.

16 Above all, taking the shield of faith, wherewith ye shall be able to quench all the fiery darts of the wicked.

17 And take the helmet of salvation, and the sword of the Spirit, which is the word of God.

18 Praying always with all prayer and supplication in the Sprit, and watching thereunto with all perseverance and supplication for all saints.

Don't allow discord, distrust, pride, rejection, misunderstanding, hatred, bitterness, unforgiveness, resentment, and strife to go undealt with in your marriage.

PROVERBS **10:12**

Hatred stirs up conflict, but love covers all offenses.

1 PETER **4:8**

8 And above all things have fervent charity among yourselves: for charity shall cover the multitude of sins.

Who are you, that you can't forgive others. I say, when people don't want to forgive, and they hold offenses. I say, "look at yourself." Because you have done wrong, and had to ask for forgiveness. So, look at it like that. You have to loose it, and let it go. You can't hold unforgiveness in your heart. You have to forgive. Unforgiveness is a blessing blocker. It will hinder your faith, and it will open the door to the enemy. Unforgiveness leads to bitterness and strife.

UNFORGIVENESS

MARK **11:24-26**

24 Therefore I say unto you, what things soever ye desire, when, ye pray, believe that ye receive them, and ye shall have them,

25 And when ye stand praying, forgive, if ye have ought against any that your father also which is in heaven may forgive you your trespasses.

26 But if ye do not forgive, neither will your Father which is in heaven forgive your trespasses.

Psalm 32:5
Proverbs 28:14
Matthew 6:14-15
Luke 6:37
Luke 17:3-4
Ephesians 4:32
Colossians 3:13
1 John 1:9

BITTERNESS

COLOSSIANS **3:19**

Husbands, love your wives and do not be embittered against them.

Proverbs 15:1
Proverbs 20:22
Acts 8:23
Romans 12:17-21
Ephesians 4:26
Ephesians 4:31
Hebrews 12:15
James 1:19-20

STRIFE

Galatians **5:15**

But if ye bite and devour one another, take heed that ye be not consumed one of another.

Proverbs 10:12
Proverbs 13:10
Proverbs 20:3
Proverbs 28:25
Proverbs 29:22
Romans 13:13
Philippians 2:3
James 3:14-16

WATCH YOUR WORDS

Ephesians 4:26, be ye angry and sin not; let not the sun go down upon your wrath. So, walk in love and understanding with one another.

Ephesians 4:29 Let no corrupt communication proceed out of your mouth, but that which is good to the use of edifying, that it may minister grace unto the hearers.

Colossians 4:6 Let your speech be always with grace, seasoned with salt, that ye may know how ye ought to answer every man.

1 Peter 3: 9 Not rendering evil for evil, or railing for railing; but contrariwise blessing. Don't retaliate with insults when you are insulted, but blessed them.

Proverbs 12:18 There is that speaketh like the piercings of a sword: but the tongue of the wise is health. (Cutting remarks)

Proverbs 15:1 A soft answer turneth away wrath; but grievous words stir up anger. (Gentle answer)

Proverbs 15:4 A wholesome is a tree of life: but perverseness therein is a breach in the spirit.

Proverbs 21:23 Whoso keepeth his mouth and his tongue keepeth his soul from troubles.

LET LOVE ABIDE

When you obey God's word you show how completely you love him. We should live our lives according to the word. We have to love unconditionally.

I JOHN 3:18

My little children, let us not love in word, neither in tongue, but in deed and in truth.

If you say you love, let it show by your actions, not only in words.

I JOHN 4:11

Beloved, if God so loved us, we ought also to love one another.

1 CORINTHIANS 13:4-7

4) Charity suffereth long, and is kind; charity envieth not; charity vaunteth not itself; is not puffed up.

5) Doth not behave itself unseemly, seeketh not her own, is not easily provoked, thinketh no evil.

6) Rejoiceth not in iniquity, but rejoiceth in the truth.

7) Beareth all things, believeth all things, hopeth all things, endureth all things.

JOHN 13:34

A new commandment I give unto you, that ye love one another; as I have loved you, that ye also love one another.

ROMANS 12:10

Be kindly affectioned one to another with brotherly love; in honour preferring one another.

1 CORINTHIANS 16:14

Let all your things be done with charity.

1 JOHN 3:18

My little children, let us not love in word, neither in tongue, but in deed and in truth.

1 JOHN 4:4-6

4 He that saith, I know him, and keepeth not his commandments, is a liar, and the truth is not in him.

5 But who keepeth his word in him verily is the love of God perfected; hereby know we that we are in him.

6 He that saith he abideth, in him ought himself also so to walk, even as he walked.

1 JOHN 4:7-8

Beloved, let us love one another: for love is of God; and every one that loveth is born of God, and knoweth God. He that loveth not knoweth not God; for God is love.

1 John 4:11

Beloved, if God so loved us, we ought also to love one another.

When you obey God's word you show how completely you love Him. We should live our lives according to the word. You have to love unconditionally.

DELIVERANCE, FEAR OF GOD AND STRONGHOLDS

There are three areas the Holy Spirit revealed to me concerning the subject of marriage.

DELIVERANCE

1) God wants to bring deliverance in your marriage.

FEAR OF GOD

2) He wants you to fear Him

STRONGHOLDS

3) He wants to break strongholds in your marriage

WALK IN LIBERTY AND FREEDOM IN YOUR MARRIAGE

JOHN 8:36

If the Son therefore shall make you free, ye shall be free indeed.

ROMANS 8:2

For the law of the Spirit of life in Christ Jesus hath made me free from the law of sin and death.

ROMANS 8:31

What then shall we say to these things? If God be for us, who can be against us.

ROMANS 8:37

Nay, in all these things we are more than conquers through him that loved us.

1 CORINTHIANS 10:13

There hath no temptation taken you but such as common to man: but God is faithful; who will not suffer you to be tempted above that ye are able; but will with the temptation also make a way to escape, that ye may be able to bear it.

I Corinthians 15:57

But thanks be to God, which giveth us the victory through our Lord Jesus Christ.

Galatians 5:1

Stand fast therefore in the liberty wherewith Christ hath made us free, and be not entangled again with the yoke of bondage.

1 John 5:4 For everyone born of God overcomes the world. This is the victory that overcomes the world, even our faith.

CHAPTER 1

DELIVERANCE

Deliverance- to change from, to free from, release, to set free.

What happens when your mind is not renewed with the word of God? It will hinder your deliverance. You will continue to function on your own way of doing things. You will continue to struggle with old habits, and old vices, You will always go back to what you got delivered from if you are not careful. It will become a cycle or pattern. Why? Because you are trying to do it your own way, and not God's way. I hear people say I just couldn't help myself. No, you can't, but with God's help you can. Don't let the enemy keep telling you that lie. It's all about your will. It's a choice. You choose to do right or wrong.

PHILIPPIANS 4:13

I can do all thing through Christ who strengthens me.

No more excuses you have help. That's why Holy Spirit is so vital in one's life.

ACT 1:8

8 but ye shall receive power after that the Holy Ghost is come upon you; and ye shall be witnesses unto men both in Jerusalem, and in all Judea, and in Samaria, and unto the uttermost part of the earth. You need help to overcome. Holy Spirit will help you pray when

you don't know what to pray, and how to pray. You might not know what to do, but Holy Spirit does.

Romans 8:26-27

26 Likewise the Spirit also helpeth our infirmities (weaknesses): for we know not what we should pray for, as we ought, but the Spirit himself maketh intercession for us with groanings which cannot be uttered.

27 And he that searcheth the heart, knoweth what is the mind of the Spirit, because he maketh intercession for the saints according to the will of God.

Situations has to be confronted, and not continued to be overlooked in the marriage. If you don't confront and acknowledge the issue will go on and on for months and years. You have to deal with it. You might not want your spouse to know that you are struggling with certain issues. It might be certain habits you are dealing with such as smoking, drinking, drugs, sexual vices; whatever the case may be. You might say what she doesn't know, want hurt. No, that's the wrong attitude to have. You should be able to share with your spouse, that's your best friend. You should feel comfortable, and be able to talk to your spouse about anything, at any time. You might say oh my spouse is not around, and will never know what I am doing. You might try to hide it, but you can't hide from God. He sees every move you make.

Proverbs 5:21

For the ways of man are before the eyes of the Lord, and he pondereth all his goings.

So be true and honest to yourself. Just be real. We all have areas we need to improve. It is very important what goes in your eye and ear gate. You might not think certain things will affect you or influence you, but it does and it will.

Psalm 101:3

I will set no wicked thing before mine eyes; I hate the work of them that turn aside; it shall not cleave to me.

So, you can't watch things that are vile and vulgar and expect it to be alright. No, it is not alright. You say I can handle it. I am strong, it will not bother me. You might not like some things your spouse says to you, but sometimes you can't see what the other person sees at the time. It is a warning from God, but you have to take heed and listen. You might not even agree with them, but eventually you will see. You might not think watching or listening to certain shows or music will impact your relationship with your spouse, but it does. Remember you live in a fleshly body, and the flesh like to be gratified. It likes pleasure and satisfaction.

Romans 8:5

For they that are after the flesh do mind the things of the flesh; but they that are after the Spirit, the things of the Spirit.

Look at Galatians 5:19-21 says about the flesh.

19) Now the works of the flesh are manifest, which are these adultery, fornication, uncleanness, lasciviousness (lustful pleasure), idolatry, witchcraft, hatred, variance (strife, discord, contention), emulations (jealousy and envy), wrath (passionate outbursts), strife, seditions, heresies (schism), envyings, murders, drunkenness, revelings (wild parties), and such like: of the which I tell you before, as I have also told you in time past, that they which do such things shall not inherit the kingdom of God.

You say I can handle it. Time will tell. What happens when temptation arise? You will see how strong you really are. Will you choose to bow to the temptation and give in? Or will you choose to resist the temptation. Remember you are dealing with the flesh. Be careful what you feed your mind and what is going in your ears. It is very important.

Psalm 19:12-13

12 Who can understand his errors? Cleanse, thou me from secret faults.

13 Keep back thy servant also from presumptuous sins; let them not have dominion over me: then shall I be upright, and I shall be innocent from the great transgression.

You have to want to be delivered from bondages that have you bound. I don't care how long you have been dealing with an issue. It's all about how bad do you want to be free and stay free. There is nothing too hard for God, and all things are possible to them that believe. God is greater than any habit, vice, lust, temptation, test or trial. You can overcome because the greater one is within you.

1 John 4:4, Ye are of God, little children, and have overcome them: because greater is he that is in you, that he that is in the world.

God is greater that any habit, vice, test or trial you encounter.

Your testimony should be the thing I used to do; I don't do anymore. Why? You should get to the point. Ok enough is enough. There is nothing too hard for God, and all things are possible to them that believe. Again, I say, God is greater than any habit, temptation, lust, vice, test or trial. You can overcome because the greater one is in you.

Prayer:

Father God, I thank you that you have delivered my spouse from the power of darkness and have translated him/her into the kingdom of your dear Son. In whom we have redemption through his blood, even the forgiveness of sins. Cleanse us from all filthiness of the flesh and spirit. Cleanse us from every wrong thought, every wrong attitude and every wrong behavior that will separate us from you, in the name of Jesus, Amen. Thank you that we standfast therefore in the liberty wherewith Christ hath made us free, and we will not be entangled again with the yoke of bondage. Thank you that you cleanse us from presumptuous sins; let them not have dominion over us; then shall we be upright, and we shall be innocent from the great transgression. In the Name of Jesus, Amen.

Psalm 19: 12, 13

12 Who can understand his error? Cleanse us from secret faults.

13 Keep back us from presumptuous sins; let them not have dominion over us then shall we be upright, and we shall be innocent from the great transgression.

Psalm 34:17

The righteous cry out, and the Lord hears them; he delivers them from all their troubles.

Romans 6:14

For sin shall not have dominion over you; for ye are not under the law, but under grace.

Galatians 5:1

Standfast therefore in the liberty wherewith Christ hath made us free, and we will not be entangles again with the yoke of bondage.

CHAPTER 2

FEAR OF GOD

Fear – reverence, due regard, respect; awe of God's power and authority.

The fear of God is having an awe of Him. We should respect Him because he is holy. So, if we respect God, we should be aware of our respect towards one another. We have to think before we speak, act and react. The fear of God is missing in many people lives, because if we feared God more, we would think before we do some of the things we do. Fear of God restrains us from sin. Fear of God is produced after you know what the word of God says. People don't fear God because they don't acknowledge the word of God. Until you really get a revelation of obeying the word of God, and the voice of God you will not fear God. You will not listen anyway when you are told to do something, or not to do something. Even when you fall short, you repent and get it right.

1 John 1:5-10

5 This then is the message which we have heard of him, and declare unto you, that God is light, and in him is no darkness at all.

6 If we say that we fellowship with him and walk in darkness, we lie, and do not the truth.

7 But if we walk in the light, as he is in the light, we have fellowship one with another, and the blood of Jesus Christ his Son cleanseth us from all sin.

8 If we say we have no sin, we deceive ourselves, and the truth is not in us.

9 If we confess our sins, he is faithful and just to forgive us our sins and to cleanse us from all unrighteousness.

10 If we say that we have not sinned, we make him a liar, and his word is not in us.

You have many that go day by day with no regard or respect for God. They do what they want to do, act how they want to act, and live how they want to live.

DEUTERONOMY 8:6

Therefore, thou shalt keep the commandments of the Lord they God, to walk in his ways, and to fear him.

Remember you have to give account for your actions, and how you live on this earth.

PHILIPPIANS 2:10-11

10 That at the name of Jesus every knee should bow of things in heaven, and things in earth, and things under the earth.

11 And that every tongue should confess that Jesus Christ is Lord, to the glory of God the Father.

PROVERBS 8:13

13 The fear of the Lord is to hate evil, pride, and arrogancy and the evil way, and the froward mouth do I hate.

So, when you fear the Lord, you will hate what he hates, and love what he loves.

1 Peter 1:16

Be ye holy, for I am holy. To the only wise God our Savior, be glory and majesty, dominion, and power, both now and ever. Amen.

Jude 1:25

Therefore, as husbands and wives we should be careful how we handle one another.

Job 6:24

Teach me, and I will hold my tongue: and cause me to understand wherein I have erred.

We have to forgive quickly, never should we keep record of one another's wrong sins and mistakes, but we are guilty of doing this often; especially, during an argument. Lord helps us!

Have you asked yourself the question. How does God feel about the way I'm treating my spouse? Do you talk to one another any kind or way? Don't ever think you are always right, and you don't see anything wrong with your actions?

Proverbs 3:7, says be not wise in thine own eyes, fear the Lord, and depart from evil.

Do you find fault in your spouse? Do you ignore your faults. Do you acknowledge when you are wrong? Remember you want respect, so you have to be respectful as well. Treat your spouse the way you want to be treated. Sometimes we can say the wrong words, and don't realize how words are hurtful. Be mindful of what you say, and how you say it. Words hurt and words matter. We are to enjoy one another.

JOHN 10:10

The thief cometh not, but for to steal, and to kill, and to destroy: I am come that they might have life, and that they might have it more abundantly.

PSALM 147:11

The Lord taketh pleasure in them that fear him, in those that hope in his mercy.

PSALM 99:5

Exalt ye the Lord our God, and worship at his footstool; for his is holy.

PSALM 112:1

Praise ye the Lord, Blessed is the man that feareth the Lord, that delighteth greatly in his commandments.

PROVERBS 9: 10,11

10 The fear of the Lord is the beginning of wisdom: and the knowledge of the holy is understanding.

11 For by me they days shall be multiplied, and the years of thy life, shall be increased.

PSALM 111:10

The fear of the Lord is the beginning of wisdom; a good understanding have all they that do his commandments; his praise endureth forever.

James 1:5

If any of you lack wisdom, let him ask of God, that giveth to all men liberally, and upbraideth not; and it shall be given him.

What is Wisdom?

Wisdom- the ability and act using knowledge, experience understanding, and insight, good judgement, wise, skill.

What is Knowledge?

Knowledge – clear and certain mental apprehension, the fact or condition of being aware of something; learning; insight; knowing.

What is Understanding?

Understanding – you know how it works, or what it means.

FEAR OF THE LORD- THE BLESSING

Reveals Covenant

Psalms 25:14

The secret of the Lord is with them that fear him; and he will shew them his covenant.

Lack Nothing

Psalm 34:9

O fear the Lord, ye his saints: for there is no want to them that fear him.

Wisdom

Psalm 111:10

The fear of the Lord is the beginning of wisdom; a good understanding have all they hat do his commandments: his praise endureth forever.

Blessed

Psalm 128:1

Blessed is every one that feared the Lord; that walketh in his ways

Desires fulfilled

PSALM 145:19

He will fulfill the desire of them that fear him: he also will hear their cry, and will save them.

Add Length to Life

PROVERBS 10:27

The fear of the Lord prolongeth days; but the uears of the wicked shall be shortened.

Secure Fortress

PROVERBS 14:26,27

26 In the fear of the Lord is strong confidence; and his children shall have a place of refuge.

27 The fear of the Lord is a fountain of life, to depart from the snares of death.

Wealth and Honour

PROVERBS 22:4

By humility and the fear of the Lord are riches, and honour, and life.

Prayer:

Father God, I thank you that you will teach us the way, O Lord, we will walk in thy truth; unite our heart to fear thy name. We will reverence you in our words and actions. We will fear the Lord our God, to walk in all his ways, and to love him, and to serve the Lord our God with all our heart and with all our soul. We will cleanse ourselves from all filthiness of the flesh and spirit, perfecting holiness in the fear of the Lord. Help us to fear you God, and we shall be blessed. In the name of Jesus, Amen.

Deuteronomy 10:12

And now, Israel, what doth the Lord thy God require of thee, but to fear the Lord thy God, to walk in all his ways, and to love him, and to serve the Lord thy God with all thy heart and with all thy soul.

Psalm 86:11

Teach me thy way, O Lord, I will walk in thy truth: unite my heart to fear they name.

2 Corinthians 7 :1

Having therefore, these promises, dearly beloved, let us cleanse ourselves from all filthiness of the flesh and spirit, perfecting holiness in the fear of God.

Psalm 112:1

Praise ye the Lord, Blessed is the man that feareth the Lord, that delighteth greatly in his commandments.

CHAPTER 3

STRONGHOLDS

You have to understand the root of the problem in order to deal with a problem. What is the bottom line why something is happening? You wander why it is so hard for certain habits and behaviors to be eradicated from someone's life. You have to deal with the stronghold. That's why it is difficult for certain individuals to be free from a certain bondages or habits.

2 Corinthians **10:4-5**

4 For the weapon of our warfare are not carnal, but mighty through God to the pulling down of strongholds.

5 Casting down imaginations, and every high thing exalteth itself against the knowledge of God and bringing into captivity every thought to the obedience of Christ.

What are strongholds? Strongholds are wrong thought patterns, and behaviors that are contrary to the word of God. A grip of sinful or unbiblical thinking; fortress. You are weaker that the thing or habit that has rule over you. You have no control over it, and you can't seem to stop doing it. You know it is wrong, but the flesh is enjoying the behavior. You say, I will repent when I am finish. No, that is the wrong attitude to have. Don't use the grace of God as an escape goat. You must realize there is no power greater than our God. The question is, How Bad Do You Want To Be Free From It?

You can be kept if you want to. No excuses. You can't use the phrase God is still working on me. Well how long will it take for you to submit your will to God's will. That is the only way for your deliverance to take place. Ask God for help.

Psalm 13:23-24

23 Search me, O God, and know my heart: try me, and know my thoughts.

24 And see if there is any wicked way in me, and lead me in the way everlasting.

2 Corinthians 12:9

And he said unto me, my grace is sufficient for thee: for my strength is made perfect in weakness.

Grace is the divine influence upon the heart and its reflection in your life. God's enabling power.

So, this tells me you can't do anything in your own strength and ability. You need help, God's grace will help you to overcome any weakness or problem in your life. You have to change your mindset. What is a mindset? It is a fixed state where your mind makes no concept for change. You enjoy doing what you are doing, even though you know it is contrary to the word of God.

Ephesians 4:22-23

22 That ye put off concerning the former conversation the old man, which is corrupt according to the deceitful lusts.

23 And be renewed in the spirit of your mind.

The renewing of your mind is the key to change within you. You have to put off the old way of thinking and embrace God's way of thinking which is according to the word of God. It goes beyond your natural and carnal mind.

PHILIPPIANS **2:5**

Let this mind be in you, which was also in Christ Jesus.

You have to discipline your mind on how to control wrong and toxic thoughts. You have to control your imaginations which is a thought and idea or reasoning, an image with a way of thinking attached to it. If the enemy can penetrate your thoughts, he can cause you to do anything with your actions. That's why you have to discipline your thoughts with the word of God. You will never change what you do, until you change the way you think.

How do you renew your mind?

1) Read the word
2) Meditate on the word
3) Confess the word
4) Apply the word

JOSHUA **1:8**

8 This book of the law shall not depart out of thy mouth; but thou shalt meditate therein day and night, that thou mayest observe to do according to all that is written therein: for then thou shalt make thy way prosperous, and then thou shalt have good success.

Prayer:

Father God, I thank you that you will break every stronghold in our lives. Help us to get rid of every wrong attitude, every wrong thought pattern, and every wrong behavior that does not please you. Help us to think right, talk right, and believe right. Thank you, Lord, that our minds are renewed according to the word of God. Let the words of our mouth and the meditation of our heart be acceptable in your sight, O Lord, my rock and my redeemer.

2 Corinthians 10:4-5

For the weapons of our warfare are not carnal, but mighty through God to the pulling down of strongholds, casting down imaginations and every high thing that exalteth itself against the knowledge of God, and bringing into captivity every thought to the obedience of Christ.

Jude 1:24-25

24 Now unto him that is able to keep you from falling, and to present you from falling, and to present you faultless before the presence of his glory with exceeding joy.

Psalm 46:1

God is our refuge and strength, a very present help in trouble.

Isaiah 43:18

You keep him in perfect peace whose mind is stayed on you, because he trusts in you.

CONFESSION OF MIND

I confess that I will no longer permit the devil to have a foothold in my mind and emotions. I am employing the use of the power of God, the weapons of the Holy Spirit, and the name of Jesus Christ. I command the devil to withdraw his lies from my mind and emotions and to flee from me. The enemy has no right to operate inside my mind, and I refuse to allow his operation in my soul to continue. I will believe right, think right, and renew my mind daily with the word of God. I am now permanently set free from lies that have controlled me for such a long time. From this moment forward I am dominated by the truth of God's word. Lies that have held me captive for so long have no more power over me uproot it now. I declare this by faith in the name of Jesus. Holy Spirit, I ask for help as I learn to utilize my weapons of my warfare that you have made available to me. In the name of Jesus, Amen,

ROMANS 12:1-2

1 I beseech you therefore, brethren, by the mercies of God, that ye present your bodies a living sacrifice, holy, acceptable unto God, which is your reasonable service.

2 And be not conformed to this world: but be ye transformed by the renewing of your mind, that ye may prove what is that good, and acceptable, and perfect, will of God.

Philippians 4:8

Finally, brethren, whatsoever things are true, whatsoever things are honest, whatsoever things are just, whatsoever things are pure, whatsoever things are lovely, whatsoever things are of good report; if there be any virtue, and if there be any praise, think on these things.

CONFESSION FOR DELIVERANCE FROM STRONGHOLDS AND HABITS

Jesus is Lord over my life. For the weapons of my warfare are not carnal, but mighty through God to the pulling down of strongholds, casting down imaginations and every high thing that exalteth itself against the knowledge of God, and bring into captivity every thought to the obedience of Christ. I pull down every demonic stronghold in my mind. Father thank you that your anointing break and destroy all yokes of bondages over my life. I ask you to destroy all curses, generational curses that have been passed down. I bind my mind, body, will and emotions to the will of God. Your word is a lamp unto my feet and a light unto my path. Father, I thank you for destroying and cancelling every assignment of the enemy against me in any way. I thank you for the blood of Jesus restores, heals, and keeps me safe. I bind every wrong ungodly pattern of thinking, desire, behavior, habit and willful sin. I confess from this day forward I am set free and delivered from unclean spirits and habits in the name of Jesus. I curse every stronghold, Satan and all of your principalities, powers, and master spirits who rule the darkness and spiritual wickedness in high places are bound from my life and loosed from your assignment against my marriage now. No longer can you operate any of your unclean spirits or habits over me. I will not become the slave of anything that exalts itself over the word of God or be brought under its power of iniquity or transgressions. I am strengthened with power in my inner man by the Holy Spirit who lives and dwells in me. I receive total freedom. I am set free and delivered now. If the Son therefore shall make you free, ye shall be free indeed. Greater is He that is in me than he that is in the world. Father, I am redeemed from every evil work. It does not, nor can it ever come again in the name of Jesus.

Job 31:1

I made a covenant with mine eyes; why then should I think upon a maid?

Psalm 101:3

I will set no wicked thing before mine eyes: I hate the work of them that turn aside; it shall not cleave to me.

AVOID SEDUCTION

Proverbs 5:1-14

1 My son, attend to my wisdom, and bow thine ear to my understanding:

2 That thou mayest regard discretion, and that thy lips may keep knowledge.

3 For the lips of a strange woman drop as a honeycomb, and her mouth is smoother than oil.

4 But her end is bitter as wormwood, sharp as a two-edged sword.

5 Her feet go down to death; her steps take hold on hell.

6 Lest thou shouldest ponder the path of life, her ways are movable, that thou canst not know them.

7 Hear me now therefore, O ye children, and depart not from the words of my mouth.

8 Remove thy way far from her, and come not nigh the door of her house.

9 Lest thou give thine honour unto others, and thy years unto the cruel:

10 Lest strangers be filled with thy wealth; and thy labours be in the house of a stranger,

11 And thou mouth as the last, when thy flesh and thy body are consumed,

12 And say, how have I hated instruction, and my heart despised reproof.

13 And have not obeyed the voice of my teachers, nor inclined mine ear to them that instructed me!

14 I was almost in all evil in the midst of the congregation and assembly.

ENJOY YOUR OWN WIFE

54

PROVERBS 15-19

15 Drink waters out of think own cistern, and running waters out of thine own well.

16 Let thy fountains be dispersed abroad, and rivers of waters in the streets.

17 Let them be only thine own, and not strangers with thee.

18 Let thy fountain be blessed: and rejoice with the wife of thy youth.

19 Let her be as the loving hind and pleasant roe, let her breasts satisfy thee at all times; and be thou ravished always with her love.

WARNING AGAINST ADULTERY

PROVERBS 6:20-35

20 My son, keep thy father's commandment, and forsake not the law of thy mother.

21 Bind them continually upon thine heart, and tie them about thy neck.

22 When thou goest, it shall lead thee; when thou sleepest, it shall keep thee; and when thou awakest, it shall talk with thee.

23 For the commandment is a lamp; and the law is light; and reproofs of instruction are the way of life

24 To keep thee from the evil woman, from the flattery of the tongue of a strange woman.

25 Lust not after her beauty in thine heart; neither let her take thee with her eyelids.

26 For by means of a whorish woman a man is brought to a piece of bread: and the adulteress will hunt for the precious life.

27 Can a man take fire in his bosom, and his clothes not be burned?

28 Can one go upon hot coals, and his feet not be burned?

29 So he that goeth in to his neighbor's wife whosoever toucheth her shall not be innocent.

30 Men do not despise a thief, if he steal to satisfy his soul when he is hungry

31 But if he be found, he shall restore sevenfold; he shall give all the substance of his house.

32 But whoso committeth adultery with a woman lacketh understanding; he that doeth it destroyeth his own soul.

33 A wound and dishonor shall he get; and his reproach shall not be wiped away.

34 For jealousy is the rage of a man: therefore, he will not spare in the day of vengeance.

35 He will not regard any ransom; neither will he rest content, though thou givest many gifts.

Certain things you should not do if you are married, and certain places you should not go alone with the opposite sex. What would it look like if you take another man or woman out to eat breakfast, lunch or dinner on a regular basis and your spouse is not around and she does not even know you are doing this. Is this right? You might be ok with it, but have you shared this with your spouse. It's not ok for your reputation as a married man or woman. Especially, if you are in ministry. What kind of example are you setting?

ROMANS **14:16**

Let not then your good be evil spoken of.

TITUS **1:15**

I know you might say unto the pure all things are pure: but unto them that are defiled and unbelieving is nothing pure; but even their mind and conscience is defiled.

Don't put yourself in certain compromising situations that causes temptation. You might say, "Oh I can handle it, or I don't see anything wrong with doing that. The saying, is if you play with fire long enough you will get burned.

- You have men and women that have wrong motives. Use wisdom. The enemy is very crafty, your motive might be pure, and right. You say, "I was just being nice." Every person doesn't think that way.

- Every man and every woman can't be trusted. Their motives are not always right. Some are bold enough to let you know. You may be thinking one way and the other person is thinking something different. Don't lead people on, and give them the wrong idea. You can tell them that you are married, and still don't care. They will try you. Don't fall for it.

- You have to deal with certain issues with the opposite sex when it comes to limitations. Let people know in a nice way that certain things just can't happen because you are married, and stand your ground and don't back down. It has nothing to do with insecurity. It has everything to do with respect and order in your marriage. If you don't deal with these issues, you are telling the other person that it's ok to keep doing what you are doing. Until the issues are addressed, it wants change.

- You should never give another man or woman privileges you don't give your spouse. Never do something for another man or woman that you have never done or will do for your spouse. Protect your character, be a man and woman of integrity.

2 CORINTHIANS 8:21

Providing for honest things, not only in the sight of the Lord, but also in the sight of man.

The word of God will bring change in our lives. You have to work the word, until it works for you. Hebrews 10:23, Let us hold fast to the profession of our faith, without wavering, for he is faithful that promised. Don't waiver, believe God that what you pray and confess will come to pass. As you pray and confess the word of God over your spouse, and marriage, thank God for favorable results. You have to allow the word of God to instruct you, encourage you, as well as correct you.

2 TIMOTHY 3:16-17

16 All scripture is given by inspiration of God, and is profitable for doctrine, for reproof, for correction, for instruction in righteousness:

17 That the man of God may be perfect, thoroughly furnished unto all good works.

The husband and wife should be able to learn from one another. Don't one person know it all.

EPHESIANS 5:21

Submitting yourselves one to another in the fear of God.

You can both give in, be agreeable, and get along with one another. It is about taking the time out and listen to the other person. Both should be able express how they feel about the situation at hand in the marriage, not to say the woman is trying to be dominant in the marriage.

Look at Genesis 21:9-14:

God approved of Sarah advise. God always approves what is right. He will never side with wrong.

9 And Sarah saw the son of Hagar the Egyptian, which she had born into Abraham, mocking,

10 Wherefore she said unto Abraham, cast out his bondwoman and her son: for the son of this bondwoman shall not be heir with my son, even with Isaac.

11 And the thing was very grievous in Abraham's sight because of his son.

12 And God said unto Abraham, let it not be grievous in thy sight because of the lad, and because of thy bondwoman; in all that Sarah hath said unto thee, hearken unto her voice, for in Isaac shall thy seed be called.

13 And also of the son of the bondwoman will I make a nation, because he is thy seed.

14 And Abraham rose up early in the morning, and took bread, and a bottle of water, and gave unto Hagar, putting it on her shoulder, and the child, and sent her away; and she departed, and wandered in the wilderness of Beersheba.

We need each other.

1 Corinthians 11:8-9,11-12

8 For the man is not of the woman; but the woman of the man.

9 Neither was the man created for the woman but the woman for the man.

11 Nevertheless neither is the man without the woman, neither the woman without the man, in the Lord.

12 For as the woman is of the man, even so is the man also by the woman, but all things of God.

HUSBAND'S COMMITMENT

1) He is to find satisfaction in his wife

Proverbs 5:19

Let her be as the loving hind and pleasant row; le their breasts satisfy thee at all times; and be thou ravished always with her love.

2) He is to find joy in his wife.

Ecclesiastes 9:9

Live joyfully with the wife whom thou lovest all the days of the life of thy vanity, which he hath given thee under the sun, all the days of thy vanity: for that is thy portion in this life, and in thy labour which thou takest under the sun.

3) He is to concern himself with meeting her unique needs.

1 Peter 3:7

Likewise, ye husbands, dwell with them according to knowledge, giving honour unto the wife, as unto the weaker vessel, and as being heirs together of the grace of life; that your prayers be not hindered.

Provers 18:21

Whoso findeth a wife findeth a good thing, and obtaineth favor of the Lord.

Ephesians 5:28

So, ought men love their wives, as their own bodies. He that loveth his wife loveth himself.

1 Corinthians 7:2-4

2 Nevertheless, to avoid fornication, let every man have his own wife, and let every woman have her own husband.

3 Let the husband render unto the wife due benevolence, and likewise also the wife unto the husband.

4 The wife hath not power of her own body, but the husband; and likewise, also the husband; and likewise, also the husband hath not power of his own body, but the wife.

Colossians 3:19

Husbands, love your wives, and be not bitter against them.

Ephesians 5:31

For this reason, a man will leave his father and mother and be united to his wife, and the two will become one flesh.

1 Corinthians 11:3

Head of man is Christ; head of woman is man.

WIFE'S COMMITMENT

1) She is to be sexually available to her husband.

1 Corinthians 7:4

The wife hath not power of her own body, but the husband.

2) She is to prepare and plan to capture her husband's heart.

Song of Songs 4:9

9 Thou has ravished my heart, my sister, my spouse, thou hast ravished my heart with one of thine eyes, with one chain of thy neck.

10 How fair is thy love, my sister, my spouse! How much better is thy love than wine! And the smell of thine ointments than all spices.

11 Thy lips, O my spouse, drop as the honeycomb: honey and mild are under thy tongue and the smell of thy garments is like the smell of Lebanon.

3) She is to be a helper to her husband.

Genesis 2:18

And the Lord God said, it is not good that the man should be alone; I will make him a help meet for him.

Ephesians 5:22

Wives submit yourselves unto your own husband, as unto the Lord.

PSALM 31:26

She opens her mouth with wisdom, and on her tongue is the law of kindness.

PROVERBS 14:1

Every wise woman buildeth her house.

PROVERBS 31:12

She will do him good and not evil all the days of her life.

PROVERBS 12:4

A virtuous woman is a crown to her husband: but she that maketh ashamed is as rottenness in his bones.

COLOSSIANS 3:18

Wives submit yourselves unto your own husband as it is fit in the Lord.

PROVERBS 31:10

Who can find a virtuous woman? for her price is far above rubies.

TITUS 2:14

That they may teach the young women to be sober, to love their husbands, to love their children.

EPHESIANS 5:33

Nevertheless, let every one of you in particular so love his wife even as himself and the wife see that she reverence her husband.

1 PETER 3:4

But let it be the hidden man of the heart, in that which is not corruptible, even the ornament of a meek and quiet spirit, which is in the sight of God of great price.

PRAYER OF AGREEMENT

It is very important that you and your spouse are on the same page, and in agreement with the same thing concerning your prayers. My spouse and I pray together as well as we both have our own personal prayer time set apart from each other. When we pray, we are in agreement with one another on certain issues. You have to talk about that with one another.

Matthew 18:19-20

19 That if two of you shall agree on earth as touching anything that they shall ask, it shall be down of them of my Father which is in heaven.

20 For where two or three are gathered together in my name, there I am in the midst of them.

PRAYER FOR SPOUSE
AND MARRIAGE

67

Father God, I cover my spouse with faith and love. We are a man/woman of wisdom, honest, integrity and truth. We walk in the fear of the Lord. We are the head, and not the tail, above only, and not beneath. We are blessed when we goest out, and come in. Everything our hands touches it prospers. We always labor fervently for one another in prayer that we stand perfect and complete in the will of God. Our love, romance, and passion increase for one another day by day. Our marriage is strong, successful, and prosperous because Jesus is Lord. We support one another. We encourage one another. We walk in unity, and in agreement with one another. We are sensitive to one another's needs and desires. The Spirit of the Lord shall rest upon us, the spirit of wisdom and understanding, the spirit of counsel and might, the spirit of knowledge and of the fear of the Lord, and shall make us of quick understanding in the fear of the Lord. In the name of Jesus, Amen.

PRAYER FOR KNOWLEDGE, WISDOM AND UNDERSTANDING

Ephesians 1:16-23

16 Cease not to give thanks for you, making mention of you in my prayers;

17 That the God of our Lord Jesus Christ, the Father of glory, may give unto you the spirit of wisdom and revelation in the knowledge of him:

18 The eyes of your understanding being enlightened; that ye may know what is the hope of his calling, and what the riches of the glory of his inheritance in the saints.

19 And what is the exceeding greatness of his power to us-ward who believe, according to the working of his mighty power.

20 Which he wrought in Christ, when he raised him from the dead, and set him at his own right hand in the heavenly places.

21 Far above all principality, and power, and might, and dominion and every name that is named, not only in this world, but also in that which is to come:

22 And hath put all things under his feet, and gave him to be the head over all things to the church.

23 Which is his body, the fulness, of him that filled all in all.

COLOSSIANS **1:9:14**

9 Father God, I do not cease to pray for my spouse, and to desire that he/she might be filled with the knowledge of his will in all wisdom and spiritual understanding.

10 That he/she might walk worthy of the Lord unto all pleasing, being fruitful in every good work, and increasing in the knowledge of God.

11 Strengthened with all might according to his glorious power unto all patience and longsuffering with joyfulness.

12 Giving thanks unto the Father, which hath made us meet to be partakers of the inheritance of the saints in light.

13 Who hath delivered us from the power of darkness, and hath translated us into the kingdom of his dear Son.

14 In whom we have redemption through his blood, even the forgiveness of sins.

In the name of Jesus, Amen.

PRAYER FOR
RESTORATION OF MARRIAGE

Father God, I come boldly to the throne of grace to receive mercy and find help in restoring our marriage. God, I stand in the gap for my spouse that you will break every demonic attack against our marriage. I declare no weapon form against us in any way shall prosper. Every lying tongue against us stops in its operation and maneuver now. I forgive my spouse for any wrong actions, against me. I release it now. God, I ask you to heal this broken marriage. Help us to submit to one another as we submit to the word of God. I rebuke all plans and plots of the enemy that will bring division and strife. The enemy comes to steal, kill and destroy, but we stand firm and say you came to give life, and life more abundantly. We will walk in love towards one another, and forgive one another as Christ has forgiven us. In the name of Jesus, Amen.

CONFESSION FOR SPOUSE

Father God, we ae the head, and not the tail, and shall be above only, and we shall not be beneath, because we hearken unto the commandments of the Lord.

Deuteronomy 28:13

Father God, we are blessed when we come in, and blessed when we go out, because God know the thoughts that he thinks toward us, thoughts of peace, and not evil, to give us an expected end

Deuteronomy 28:6

Jeremiah 29:11

Father God, we find favor and good understanding in the sight of God, and man because we trust in the Lord with all our heart and lean not to our own understanding therefore we acknowledge God and he directs our paths.

Proverbs 3:4-6

Father God, we will have no good thing withheld from us because we walk upright God blesses us because we trusted in the Lord.

Psalm 84:11,12

Father God, now thanks be unto God which always causeth us to triumph in Christ, and maketh manifest the saviour of his knowledge by us in every place.

2 Corinthians 2:14

Father God, we will be instructed by God and teach us in the way which we shall go and will guide us.

Psalm 32:8

Father God, cause us to hear thy lovingkindness in the morning, for in thee do we trust: cause us to know the way wherein we should walk; for we lift up our soul unto thee. Teach us to do thy will; for thou are our God: thy spirit is good; lead us into the land of uprightness.

Psalm 143:8-10

Father God, we put on therefore, as the elect of God (chosen people), holy and beloved, bowels of mercies (compassion), kindness, humbleness of mind, meekness, longsuffering. Forbearing one another, and forgiving one another, if any man have a quarrel against any; even as Christ forgave you, so also do ye.

Colossians 3:12-13

CONFESSION FOR MARRIAGE

I confess that our marriage is like a tree planted by the rivers of water that bring forth fruit in its season, shall not wither, and whatsoever we do in our marriage shall prosper.

PSALM 1:3

I confess that our marriage is unified together as one, there is no division between us. We are perfectly joined together in the same mind, and in the same judgment.

1 CORINTHIANS 1:10

I confess there is no bitterness, wrath, anger and clamour, and evil speaking toward one another.

EPHESIANS 4:31

I confess that no weapon that is formed against our marriage shall be able to prosper against us in any way. And every word that is spoken against us shall fall to the ground. For this is the heritage that we have as a servant of the Lord.

ISAIAH 54:17

I confess that we are kind to each other, affectionate toward one another, in love with each other, and we honor and respect one another.

Romans 12:10

I confess that we speak the same thing (walk in unity), and there is no division among us. I confess that we also perfectly joined together in the same mind (walking in agreement) and the same spirit.

I Corinthians 1:10

I confess that it is God's desire for us to prosper in our marriage and have a successful and healthy relationship even as we prosper spiritually.

3 John 1:2

I confess that we are kind one to another, tenderhearted, forgiving one another, even as God for Christ's sake hath forgiven you.

Colossians 4:6

PRAYER FOR GOD'S MERCY

PSALM 86:1-7,10,11,13,15

1 Bow down thine ear, Oh Lord hear me: for I am poor and needy.

2 Preserve my soul; for I am holy: o thou my God, save thy servant that trusteth in thee.

3 Be merciful unto me, I Lord: for I cry unto thee daily.

4 Rejoice the soul of thy servant, for unto thee, I Lord, do lift up my soul.

5 For thou, Oh Lord, art good, and ready to forgive our trespasses sending them away letting them go completely and forever; and plenteous in mercy unto all them that call upon thee.

6 Give ear, O Lord unto my prayer; and attend to the voice of my supplications.

7 In the day of my trouble I will call upon thee: for thou wilt answer me.

10 For thou are great and doest wondrous things: for thou are God alone.

11 Teach me thy way, O Lord; I will walk in thy truth: unite my heart: and I glorify thy name for evermore.

13 For great is thy mercy toward me: and thou hast delivered my soul from the lowest hell.

15 But thou, O Lord, art a God full of compassion, and gracious, longsuffering, and plenteous in mercy and truth.

My prayer is I have helped you in areas that will improve, and cause you to enhance in areas of your marriage, and have answered some of your questions. The three areas that I have shared is not all the answers, but it is what God shared with me concerning the subject of marriage. Remember all our dealings with God is by faith. May your marriage grow and prosper in the name of Jesus. Amen.

HEBREWS 11:6

But without faith it is impossible to please him for he that cometh to God must believe that he is, and that he is a rewarder of them that diligently seek him.

God Bless